MY BUTT IS SO PUZZLING!

Awesome Activities

Betsy Ochester
Based on the bestselling series by **Dawn McMillan**
Illustrated by **Ross Kinnaird**

Dover Publications
Garden City, New York

Answers start on page 55!

I woke up this morning looking for puzzles to do.
I craved mazes and codes and word searches, too.
My butt started bouncing; it knew the drill.
We had pages and pages and pages to fill!
So I wrote this book, and my butt helped, too.
We wanted to make super fun puzzles for you!
If the puzzles are tricky, and it's answers you seek,
they're at the back of the book —
but try not to peek!

Text copyright © 2024 by Betsy Ochester
Illustrations copyright © 2024 by Ross Kinnaird
Published work copyright © 2024 by Oratia Books
All rights reserved.

This Dover edition, first published in 2024, is an unabridged republication of the work to be published in 2024 as *I Need a New Bum! Activity Book* by Oratia Books Ltd., Auckland, New Zealand. The work is based on the series by Dawn McMillan.

International Standard Book Number
ISBN-13: 978-0-486-85321-5
ISBN-10: 0-486-85321-7

Manufactured in China
85321701   2024
www.doverpublications.com

SEEING DOUBLE

How does my butt solve puzzles? To find out, cross off all the pairs of matching letters. Then write the remaining letters in order from left to right and top to bottom in the spaces below.

BB	QQ	IT	RR	TT	KK	LL
KN	OO	JJ	XX	FF	OW	AA
HH	SS	SH	EE	MM	NN	ZZ
VV	OW	CC	DD	UU	TO	BB
RR	GG	WW	CR	TT	LL	PP
AC	II	QQ	KK	KT	HH	AA
ZZ	HE	CC	MM	EE	OO	RR
JJ	TT	CO	SS	GG	DE	EE

How does my butt solve puzzles?

I T   K N O W S

H O W   " T O   C R

A C K   T H E   C O D E !

DUNE IT RIGHT

My butt is so speedy! But will it be fast enough to reach the bottom of the sand dune — and my camel — before the sun goes down? Slide on in and help me reach the finish line.

A BUTT IN SHINING ARMOR

Which of these knight butts is the right butt? Find the one picture that matches the real me.

The Real Me!

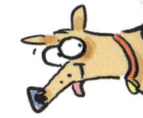

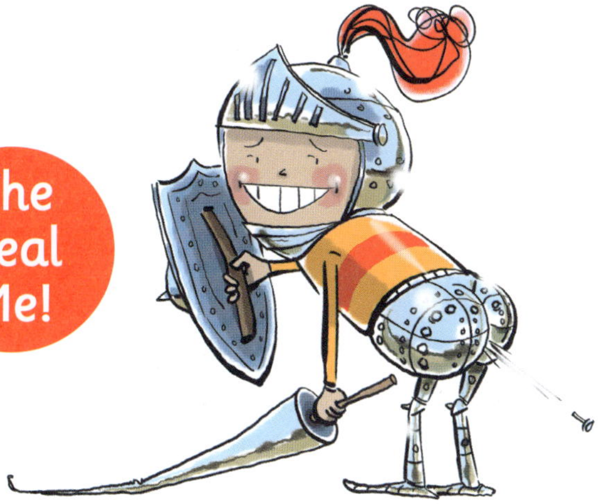

1

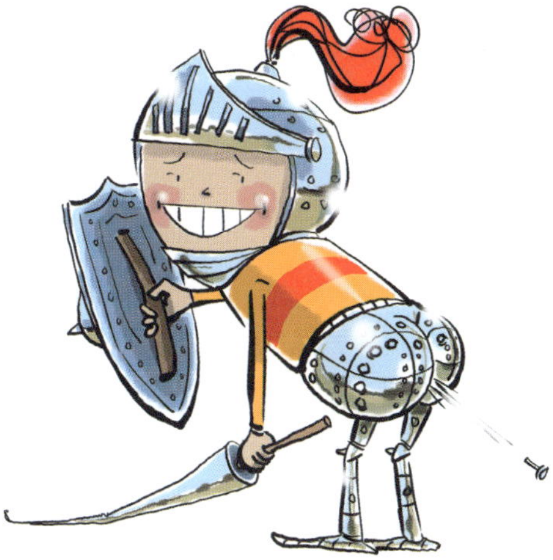

2

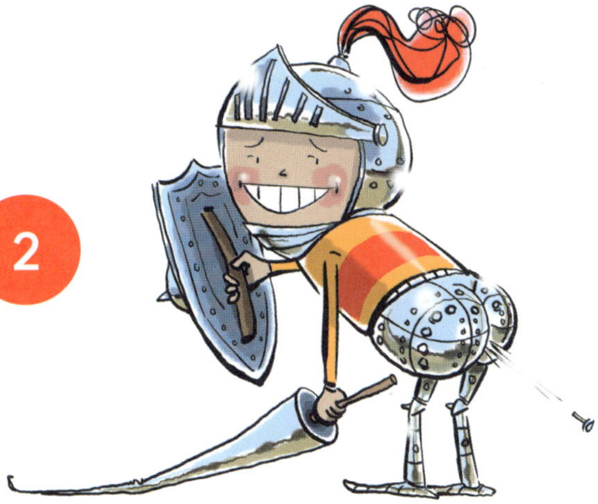

3

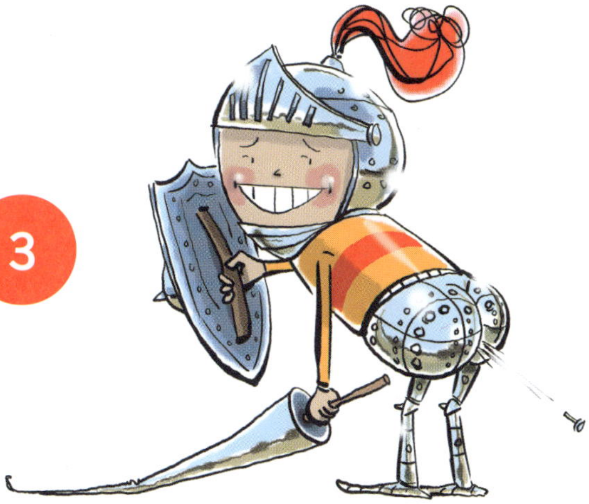

4

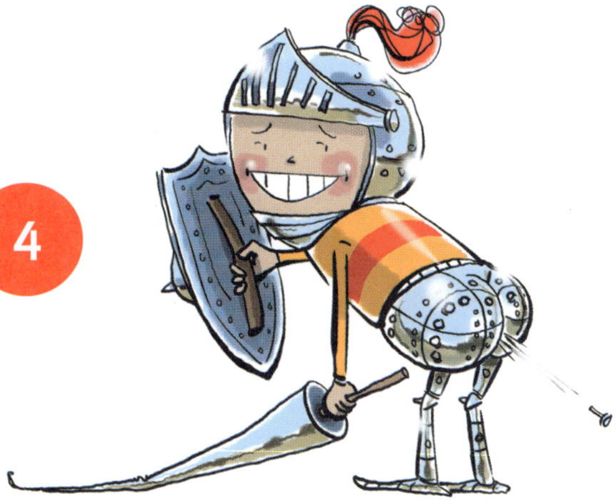

5

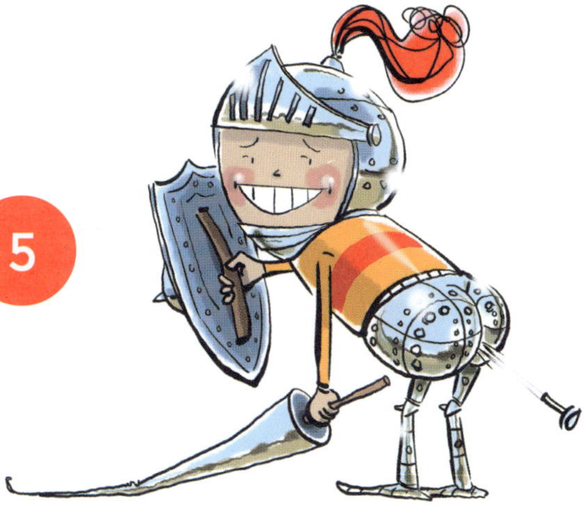

DOGGONE FUNNY

My dog is the funniest! See for yourself. Use his secret code to fill in the letters and find the answers to these *pawsome* jokes.

DOG CODE

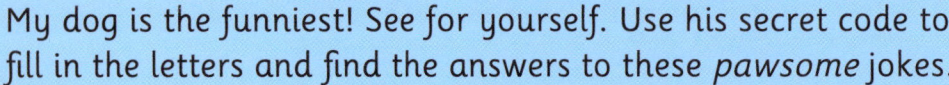

1. What do you get when you cross a dog and a dinosaur?

   _ _ _ _ _ _ _ _   _ _ _ _

2. What do lazy dogs like to do?

   _ _ _ _ _ _

   _ _ _ _ _

3. What does a dog call its father?

   _ _ _ - _ _ _

4. What did the dog say when it sat on sandpaper?
   " _ _ _ _ _ - _ _ _ _ _ !"
   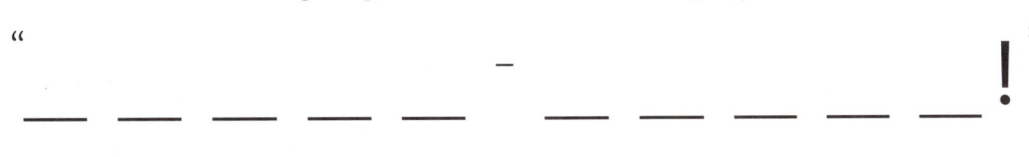

SPOT THE DIFFERENCES

My butt loves to make music! Can you find 20 differences between these two pictures of my Sound-System Backside?

WHAT'S IN A WORD?

HINDQUARTERS is a fancy word for butt! Its letters can spell lots of smaller words. Use the clues to come up with some of them. I did one to get you started.

HINDQUARTERS

REMEMBER, USE ONLY THESE LETTERS TO FILL IN THE BLANKS!

1. It rises and shines in the East. S U N
2. Female chicken. ___ ___ ___
3. Acorn or pistachio. ___ ___ ___
4. Fish often found in a can. ___ ___ ___ ___ ___
5. My uncle's wife is my ___. ___ ___ ___ ___
6. The part of a chair for your butt. ___ ___ ___ ___
7. Song sung by two people. ___ ___ ___ ___
8. ___ or shine. ___ ___ ___ ___
9. It twinkles in the night sky. ___ ___ ___ ___
10. Opposite of over. ___ ___ ___ ___ ___
11. Symbol of Valentine's Day. ___ ___ ___ ___ ___
12. It might have a caboose. ___ ___ ___ ___ ___
13. Garbage or rubbish. ___ ___ ___ ___ ___
14. It has four equal sides. ___ ___ ___ ___ ___ ___
15. Lightning's loud partner. ___ ___ ___ ___ ___ ___ ___

BOUNCING BUTT

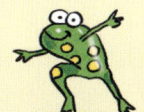

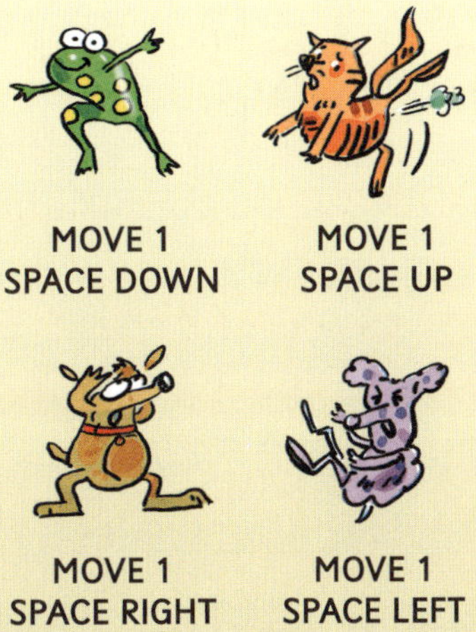
MOVE 1 SPACE DOWN
MOVE 1 SPACE UP
MOVE 1 SPACE RIGHT
MOVE 1 SPACE LEFT

My butt is so bouncy! I need to sit down. Can you help me find the right path to bounce into my dad's comfy chair? The animals will tell you which way to move.

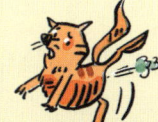

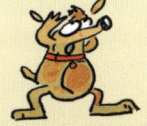

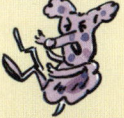

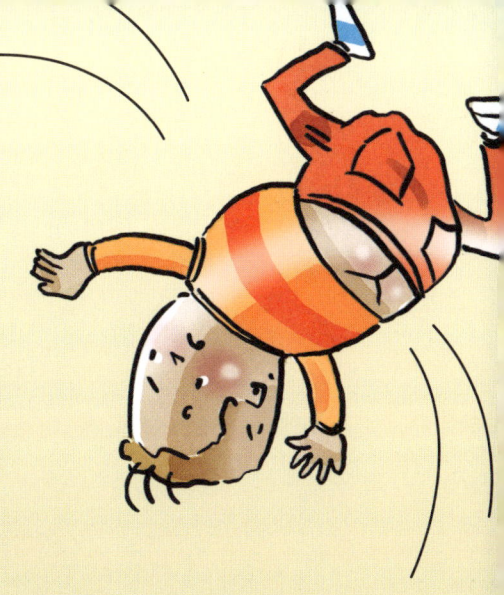

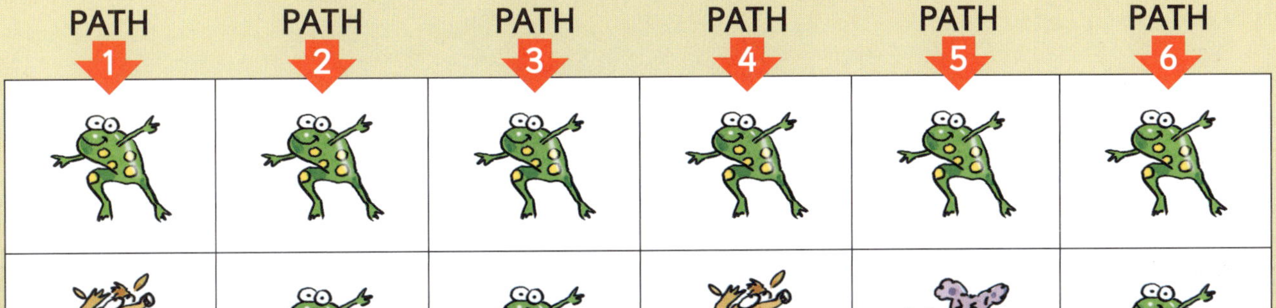
PATH 1
PATH 2
PATH 3
PATH 4
PATH 5
PATH 6

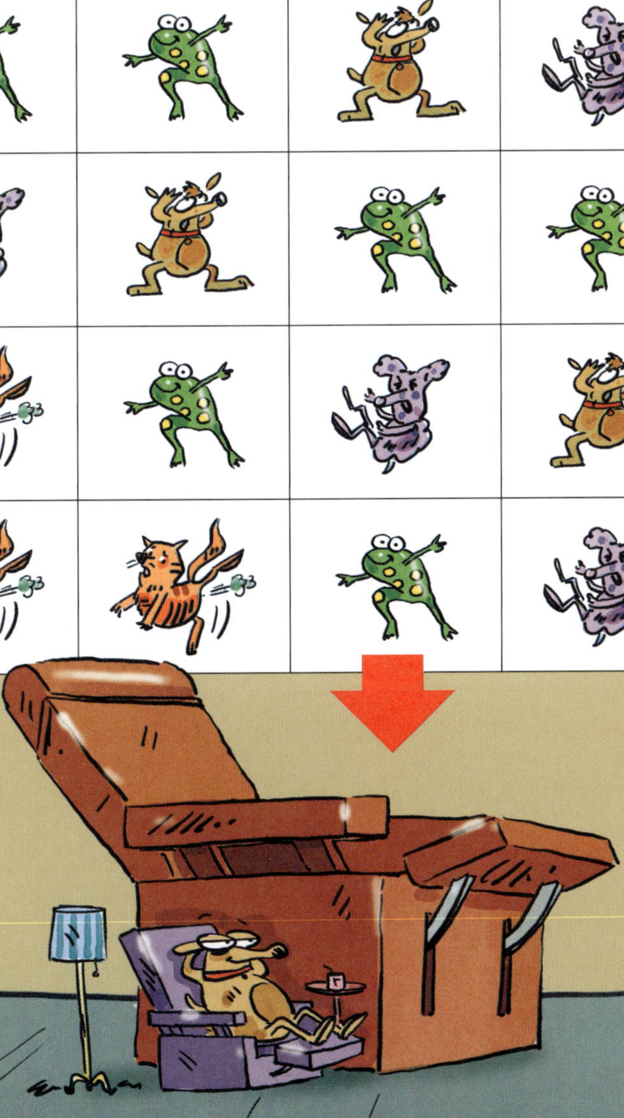

MY BUTT SOUNDS LIKE ...

My butt is almost famous! Its noises are in the movies. Here are 27 sounds it can make! Can you find each one hidden in the grid on the next page? Look up, down, across, and diagonally. I circled one to get you started. Once you've found them all, write the leftover letters in order from left to right and top to bottom. They'll spell the title of the next movie I'm making sound effects for!

ALARM CLOCK
BACON SIZZLING
BEE SWARM
BIKE HORN
CAT PURRING
CLAPPING
COUGH
DRUM
DUCK QUACKING
GIGGLE
GONG
GUITAR
LAWN MOWER
OPERA SINGER
OWL HOOTING
PHONE RINGING
PIANO
PIG SQUEALING
PLANE
RAINDROPS
ROCKET
SEAL BARKING
SNEEZE
THUNDER
TORNADO
TRAIN WHISTLE
VIOLIN

```
P L A N E R E W O M N W A L S
S P O R D N I A R S U T M N E
P S B O W K C O L C M R A L A
H O N A W H C C I T A A D P L
O P N E C K T E O W A I U I B
N E I N E O D R S U T N C G A
E R L T H Z N E G E G W K S R
R A O S E A E S U N V H Q Q K
I S I E D B N T I S E I U U I
N I V O C R H P T Z E S A E N
G N I R R U P T A C Z T C A G
I G T O N A I P R S M L K L G
N E E D L G I G G L E E I I N
G R E C L B I K E H O R N N O
L R S O W L H O O T I N G G G
```

What is the title of the next movie I'm making sound effects for?

___ ___ ___ ___ ___   ___ ___ ___ ___ ___ ___ ___   ___ ___ ___ ___

___ ___ ___   ___ ___ ___ ___ ___ ___   ___ ___ ___ ___ ___ ___ ___ ___

___ ___ ___   ___ ___ ___ ___ ___ ___

3, 2, 1... BLAST OFF!

I'm about to explore a brand-new planet! What do you think I'll see there? An alien with four butts? A space tiger? Draw your ideas here.

SPIN ON IN!

My butt is so silly! It wants to spin around this puzzle. Use the clues to fill in the spaces on the right. And here's a fun twist: the last letter of each word is also the first letter of the next word. Use the linking letters to help you spin to the center. I did the first one to get you started.

1. Shape of a circle.
5. One of the world's most popular pets.
7. Grandpa's wife is my _____.
13. The fourth month of the year.
17. Yellow citrus fruit.
21. You smell with this.
24. Animal with a trunk.
31. Ten plus ten.
36. 365 days.
39. Bunny.
44. The T in a BLT sandwich.
49. Atlantic or Pacific.
53. The eleventh month of the year.
60. Dried grapes.
66. Ewes and rams.
70. The capital of France.
74. The first day of the weekend.
81. The day before today.
89. You might do this when you're sleepy.
92. The only planet that starts with the letter N.
98. A chicken lays this.

SPOT THE DIFFERENCES

My butt is so speedy! How quickly can you spot the 10 differences between these two pictures?

BIKE CRACK-UP

Crack this simple code to learn the answer to one of my favorite jokes! First, circle every letter that's immediately to the right of a B. Then write the circled letters, from top to bottom, in the spaces below to see the answer.

What is a biker's least favorite ice-cream flavor?

```
D A V P Z B R H C Q X
L T O K Y T N M W E A
T Q M B O Y V C G R P
U P R H X K J B C W L
Y T C O X A U K F D E
X B K N C S I G E T N
C P Q A G N B Y C S P
B R E G L Z A I J X Y
R P M C A K T B O Z W
G R P V B A I X Y J H
C P W H Q N M B D O K
```

Write the circled letters here:

__ __ __ __ __   __ __ __ __

20

MATCH THE UNDIES

My dad's underwear is out to dry in the sun! Each pair of underwear has a pair that looks just like it. Can you find all 6 matching pairs?

I'M HAVING A "T" PARTY!

The word BUTT has 2 Ts and so does the word BOTTOM! I made this list of other fun double-T words. Can you figure them out? I did the first one to get you started.

1. A room at the top of a house.   <u>A</u> T T <u>I</u> <u>C</u>

2. Opposite of big.   __ __ T T __ __

3. Good, _____, best.   __ __ T T __ __

4. A baby cat.   __ __ T T __ __

5. Spread this on toast.   __ __ T T __ __

6. Garbage by the side of the road.   __ __ T T __ __

7. A bunch of cows on a ranch or a farm.   __ __ T T __ __

8. Underwear can be made of this soft material.   __ __ T T __ __

9. You might boil tea water in this.   __ __ T T __ __

10. The alphabet has 26 of these.   __ __ T T __ __

11. The three little kittens have lost their _____.   __ __ T T __ __ __

12. Use these to close your shirt.   __ __ T T __ __ __

MAKE YOURSELF HOPPY

Jump on in and match each frog joke to its answer! Each question on the left has one answer on the right. Write the correct number in each space.

What kind of cars do frogs drive? A. ____

Why do frogs make good outfielders? B. ____

What do stylish frogs wear? C. ____

What did the bus driver say to the frog? D. ____

What is a frog's favorite song? E. ____

What do you get when you cross a pig with a frog? F. ____

What do you call a frog who's stuck in the mud? G. ____

What's a frog's favorite snack? H. ____

1. Jumpsuits

2. "Head, Shoulders, Knees, and Toads"

3. Hop rods

4. French flies and a diet croak

5. Because they never miss a fly!

6. Unhoppy

7. A ham-phibian

8. "Hop on!"

MY BUTT WORE WHAT?!?

My butt has worn many, **many** things! I put together a list of 25 of my favorites. Can you put them into the grid? They'll fit in only one way. Use the number of letters in each word as a clue to where it might fit. I did one to get you started. When you're done, write the shaded letters in the spaces from top to bottom to answer my riddle!

4 Letters
KITE
TRAY

5 Letters
ARMOR
BANJO
~~BELLS~~
KAYAK
MURAL
WINGS

6 Letters
HANDLE
LIGHTS
ROCKET
WHEELS

7 Letters
COCONUT
DRUM KIT

8 Letters
BALLOONS
FEATHERS
RED PANTS

9 Letters
CAR BUMPER
COWBOY HAT
GOLD MEDAL
JET ENGINE
ROBOT LEGS

11 Letters
SOUND SYSTEM

16 Letters
GREAT GLOBS OF GLUE
ROLLER COASTER CAR

What do clouds wear on their butts?

_ _ _ _ _ _ _ _ _ - _ _ _ _ _ !

SPOT THE DIFFERENCES

Having a robo-butt would be awesome! Can you find 15 differences between these two pictures without any help from a robot?

I BROKE MY _____
NOUN

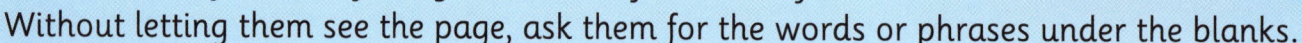

I broke my butt, and it's almost gone! I need your help to finish my song! Help me write "The Broken Butt Blues." Ask a friend or family member to join in the fun. Without letting them see the page, ask them for the words or phrases under the blanks.

Noun: a person, place, or thing **Verb:** an action word **Adjective:** a describing word

---

Yesterday, I slipped on a pile of _____ (COLOR) _____ (SOMETHING STINKY, PLURAL). Yuck!

And now, my butt looks like a squashed _____ (NAME OF A FOOD). Just my luck!

My poor butt is so _____ (ADJECTIVE). I can't even _____ (VERB) on my chair.

My cousin is showing me how perfect his _____ (BODY PART) is. It isn't fair!

What should I do? I tried to put it back together with _____ (A LIQUID).

I tried to build a new one with _____ (HIGH NUMBER) _____ (PLURAL NOUN).

But nothing worked. So, I went to see Doctor _____ (SPOOKY WORD).

She said, "The only cure is to eat a dozen helpings of _____ (YOUR LEAST FAVORITE FOOD)."

"No, thanks!" I jumped on my _____ (OBJECT WITH WHEELS) and left in a flash.

It was like in _____ (SCHOOL SUBJECT) class when I ran the _____ (LOW NUMBER)-yard dash.

When I got back to my _____ (ADJECTIVE) house, I had a(n) _____ (ADJECTIVE) thought!

I grabbed a big _____ (SOMETHING SOFT) from the couch Mom just bought.

I tied it onto my _____ (BODY PART). It worked! My butt was okay!

I _____ (VERB ENDING IN -ED) out the door. "_____ (GREETING), world! Let's play!"

PUP ART

My dog is the best! Want to draw him? Just follow these steps!

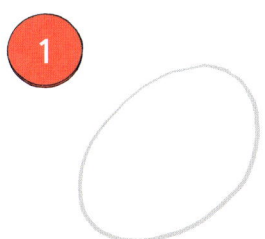
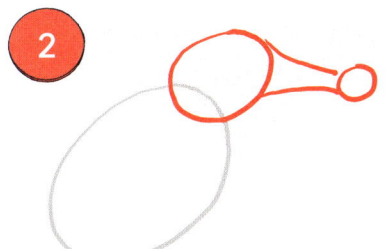

THE PERFECT BUTT

I've considered all kinds of butts for myself. Here's a list of 22 types I've dreamed about. Can you find each one in the grid? Look up, down, across, and diagonally. I circled one to get you started. Which one is your favorite?

ARTY-FARTY
BLUE
CHECKED
CHROME
FIREPROOF
FLORAL
GOLDEN
GREEN
NOISY
PINK
PLASTIC

PURPLE DOTTED
SILLY
SPARKLY
SPEEDY
SPOOKY
SQUARE
STRIPED
SUPERSONIC
TIN
TITANIUM
YELLOW SPOTTED

```
V D G O L D E N G Q W C M
C E D E K C E H C C Z H L
I T X F E L Y P C S F R N
T T S T I T A N I U M O X
S O G U Y R A R G R C M Q
A P U R P L E D O T T E D
L S E Q E E L P T L P S S
P W G E U E R I R V F P P
X O F L D I N S S O A E O
D L B T C Y O A O R O N O
J L O B C P I N K N X F K
F E R A U Q S L C A I M Y
O Y T R A F Y T R A R C L
```

31

QUACKING UP

My butt is so funny! It wrote a joke. Cross off every word that rhymes with FART. When you're done, write the leftover words in the spaces provided, in order from left to right and top to bottom, to see the joke. I found the first word for you.

PART	START	WHAT	DART	CHART	MART
CART	DO	HEART	SMART	ART	TART
PART	BART	YOU	CHART	START	CALL
MART	A	TART	CART	HEART	ART
BART	PART	CART	DUCK	START	CHART
THAT	DART	MART	PART	SMELLS	ART
PART	BAD	CART	CHART	SMART	HEART
DART	A	PART	TART	BART	FOUL
TART	ART	CHART	FOWL	HEART	PART

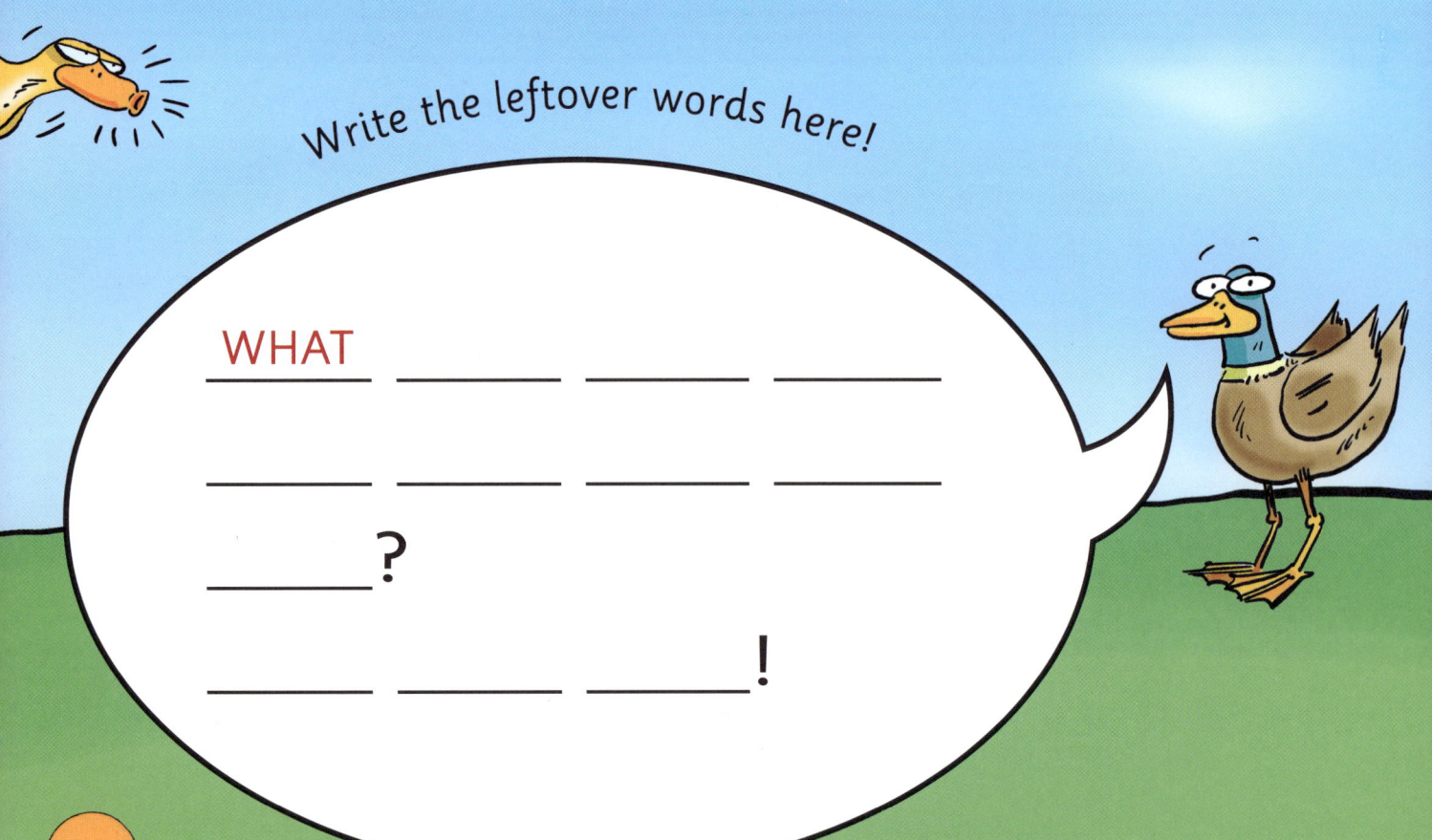

Write the leftover words here!

WHAT DO YOU CALL

A DUCK THAT SMELLS

BAD ?

A FOUL FOWL !

MATCHING MASTERPIECES

Each of my arty-farty butts has an exact match! Draw lines to connect the matching butts.

KEEP YOUR EYE ON THE BALL

MOVE 1 SPACE DOWN

MOVE 1 SPACE UP

MOVE 1 SPACE RIGHT

MOVE 1 SPACE LEFT

Can you help me make my perfect serve? The tennis balls will tell you which way to move.

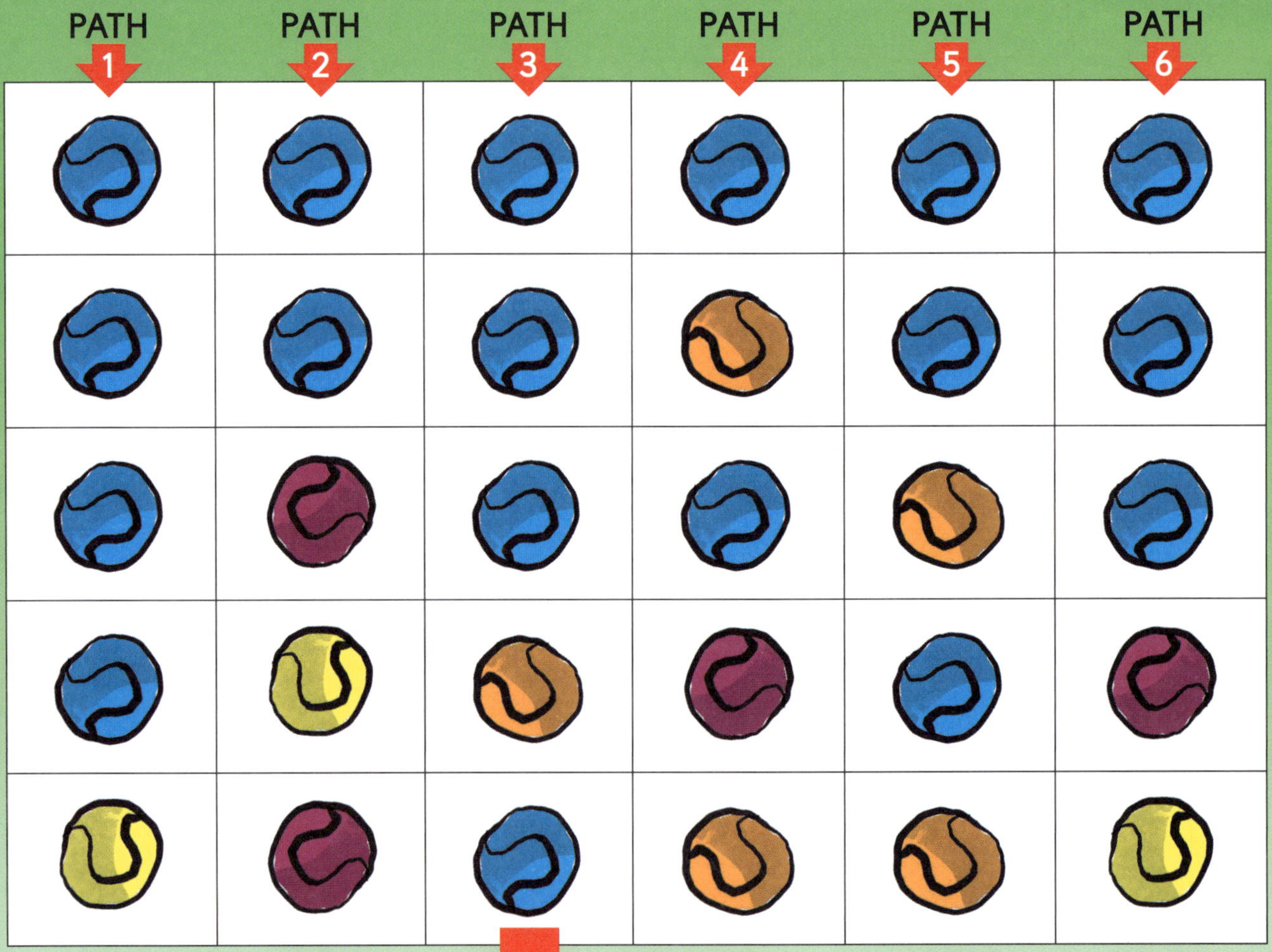

PATH 1 | PATH 2 | PATH 3 | PATH 4 | PATH 5 | PATH 6

FAMILY TIME

My cousins are having a noisemaking contest, and I'm the judge. Use the clues to figure out what each cousin had for lunch and where they placed in the contest.

Use the chart to keep track of your answers. Put an X in each box that can't be true. Put an O in boxes that match. I've filled in the information from the first clue to get you started.

	Tuna Surprise	Chicken Noodle Soup	Ham	Stew	1st Place	2nd Place	3rd Place	4th Place
Cam								
Tom								
Alexander			X	X				
Ben								

✓ 1. Alexander never eats a food with less than 3 syllables.
2. Cam, who got 3rd, only eats foods that rhyme with his name.
3. The winner, not Alexander, had chicken noodle soup for lunch.
4. Ben, who placed lower than Alexander, had stew.

SPOT THE DIFFERENCES

Join the fun! Can you find 20 differences between these two pictures of my butt-sliding friends?

BONUS ACTIVITY

Which friend is *not* butt-sliding today?

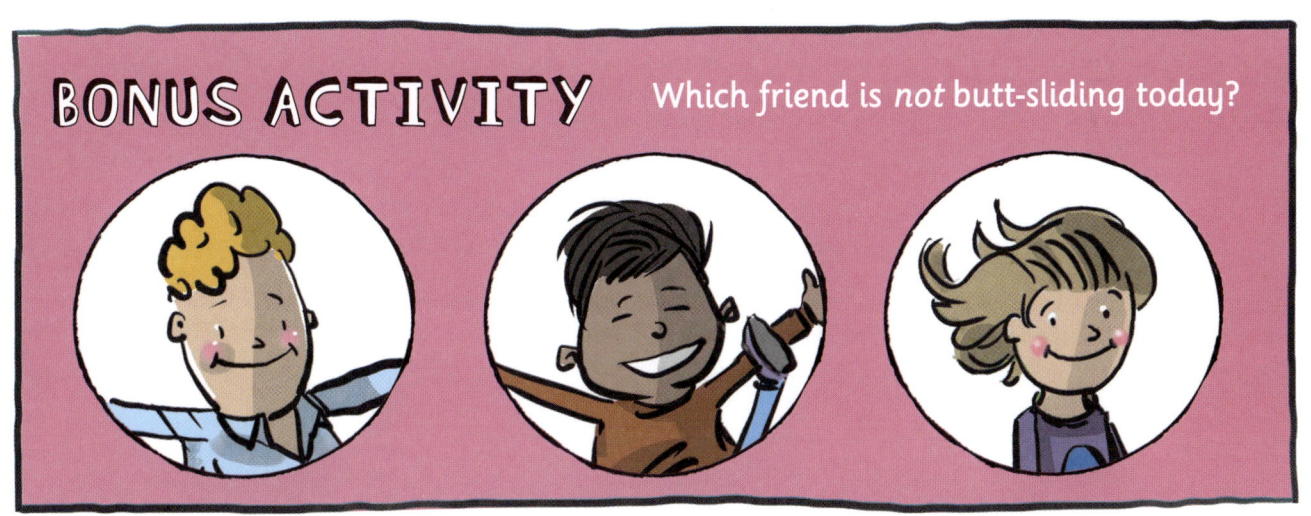

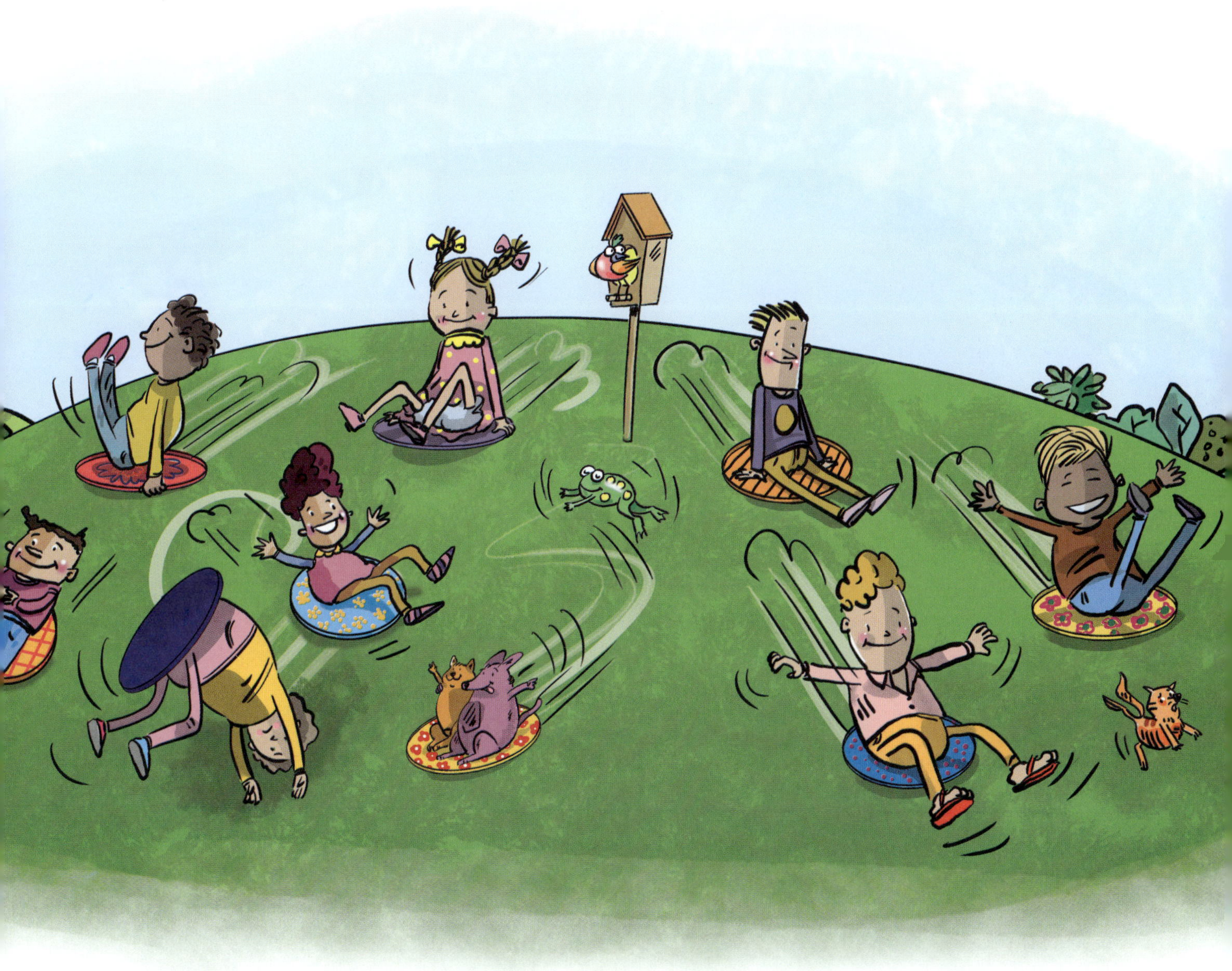

WHAT'S IN A WORD?

POSTERIOR is another fancy word for butt! Its letters can spell lots of smaller words. Use the clues to come up with some of them. I did one to get you started!

POSTERIOR

REMEMBER, USE ONLY THESE LETTERS TO FILL IN THE BLANKS!

1. As easy as ___. P I E
2. Climb from bottom to ___.
3. Your feet have ten of these.
4. A type of flower with thorns.
5. Opposite of rich.
6. One stair in a staircase.
7. You can mail a letter at the ___ office.
8. A band with three members.
9. You can't drive if one of these is flat.
10. A group of Girl Scouts or Boy Scouts.
11. Baseball, basketball, or golf.
12. A supermarket or toy shop.
13. You might hang this on your bedroom wall.
14. One of many on a zebra.
15. Male chicken.

RUNNING JOKES

Race on in and match each joke about running to its answer! Each question on the left has one answer on the right. Write the correct number in each space.

What did the two strings do in a race? A. ____

What's the best thing to drink before a marathon? B. ____

How does a bottle of glue run? C. ____

What's harder to catch the faster you run? D. ____

How do fireflies start a race? E. ____

Which runner won the race? F. ____

How did the two giraffes finish their race? G. ____

Why was the girl running around her bed? H. ____

1. At a slow paste.

2. "Ready, set, glow!"

3. Running water.

4. The one in front!

5. Neck and neck!

6. They tied.

7. She was trying to catch some sleep.

8. Your breath.

FULL OF BEANS

Bonus! I also hid the word BUTT 5 times. Can you find each one?

Beans help me go fast! Here's a list of 20 of my favorite types of beans. Can you find each one in the grid? Instead of the word "bean," you will find this: 🫘. Search up, down, across, and diagonally. It will "bean" fun! I did the first one to get you started.

- ~~BAKED BEAN~~
- BLACK BEAN
- CANNELLINI BEAN
- CRANBERRY BEAN
- FAVA BEAN
- GARBANZO BEAN
- GREAT NORTHERN BEAN
- GREEN BEAN
- JELLY BEAN
- KIDNEY BEAN
- LIMA BEAN
- MUNG BEAN
- NAVY BEAN
- PINK BEAN
- PINTO BEAN
- PURPLE STRING BEAN
- RED BEAN
- SCARLET RUNNER BEAN
- SOYBEAN
- YELLOW BEAN

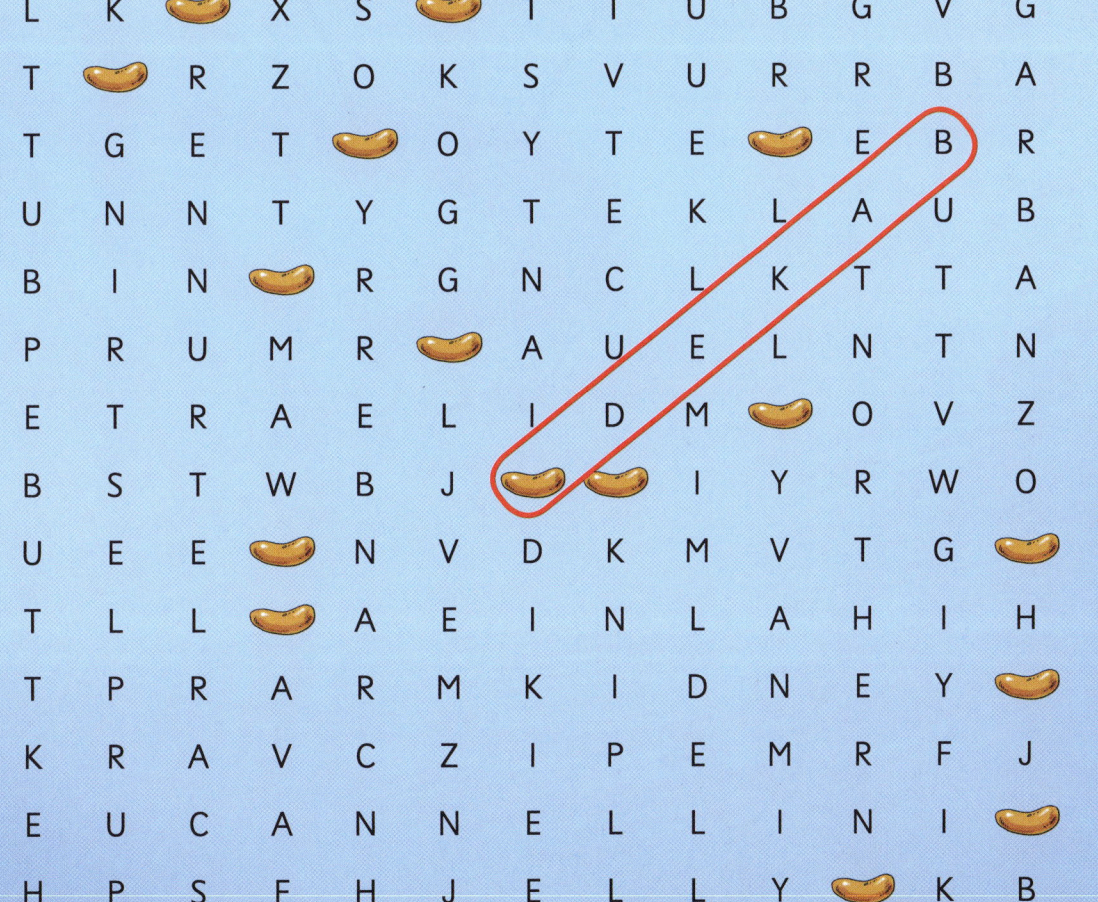

FULL OF HOT AIR

I've got a new butt! Is it a bird? Is it a plane? No — it's a hot-air balloon! Connect the dots to finish it, and then color it in.

FIND THE BLOOPERS!

BUTTOCKS is another way to say *butt.* Can you find the 3 times it's misspelled here?

BUTTOCKS	BUTTOCKS	BUTTOCKS	BUTTOCKS
BUTTOCKS	BUTTOCKS	BUTTOCKS	BUTTOCKS
BUTTOCKS	BUTTOCKS	BUTTOCKS	BUTTOCKS
BUTTOCKS	BUTTOCKS	BUTTOCKS	BUTTOCKS
BUTTOCKS	BUTTOCKS	BUTTOCKS	BOTTOCKS
BUTTOCKS	BUTTOCKS	BUTTOCKS	BUTTOCKS
BUTTOCKS	BUTTOCKS	BUTTOCKS	BUTTOCKS
BUTTOCKS	BUTTOCKS	BUTTOCKS	BUTTOCKS
BUTTOCKS	BUTTOCKS	BUTTOCKS	BUTTOCKS
BUTTOCKS	BUTTOCKS	BUTTOCKS	BUTTOCKS
BUTTOCKS	BUTTOCKS	BUTTOCKS	BUTTOCKS
BUTTOCKS	BUTTOCKS	BUTTOCKS	BUTTOCKS
BUTTOCKS	BUTTOCKS	BUTTOCKS	BUTTOCKS
BUTTOCKS	BUTTOCKS	BUTTOCKS	BUTTOCKS
BUTTOCKS	BUTTOCKS	BUTTOCKS	BUTTOCKS
BUTTOCKS	BUTTOCKS	BUTTCCKS	BUTTOCKS
BUTTOCKS	BUTTOCKS	BUTTOCKS	BUTTOCKS
BUTTOCKS	BUTTOCKS	BUTTOCKS	BUTTOCKS
BUTTOCKS	BUTTOCKS	BUTTOCKS	BUTTOCKS
BUTTOCKS	BUTTOCKS	BUTTOCKS	BUTTOCKS
BUTTOCKS	BUTTOCKS	BUTTOCKS	BUTTOCKS
BUTTOCKS	BUTTOCKS	BUTTOCKS	BUTTOCKS
BUTTOCKS	BUTTOCKS	BUTTOCKS	BUTTOCKS
BUTTOCHS	BUTTOCKS	BUTTOCKS	BUTTOCKS
BUTTOCKS	BUTTOCKS	BUTTOCKS	BUTTOCKS

SUPER CODE

It's time to use your superhero code-cracking skills! Use the clues to write one letter in each square. When you're done, read across to find the two-word answer to this joke:

What do you call a superhero who fights for computers?

1. The second letter in CAPE.
2. The letter that appears the most times in SASSAFRAS.
3. The letter that sounds like the word SEA.
4. The letter that's 3 letters after O in the alphabet.
5. The sixth letter in DAYDREAM.
6. The fifth letter in the alphabet.
7. The letter that's in both UNDER and BIN.
8. The eighth letter from the end of the alphabet.
9. The letter that's in BARK but not in BRICK.
10. The letter that is 5 letters after Q in the alphabet.
11. The letter that appears the most times in BEEKEEPER.
12. The middle letter of MEERKAT.

Use this to help with some of the clues!

A B C D E F G H I J K L M N O P Q R S T U V W X Y Z

Write the answers here:

SEEING DOUBLE

Why can't two elephants go swimming at the same time? To find out, cross off all the pairs of matching letters. Then write the remaining letters, in order from left to right and top to bottom, in the spaces below.

LL	BE	JJ	QQ	CA	RR	TT
US	MM	DD	ET	NN	OO	PP
HH	HE	KK	TT	UU	ZZ	YO
WW	TT	VV	AA	NL	XX	CC
SS	YH	GG	AV	BB	II	EO
CC	RR	NE	KK	AA	PA	WW
IR	EE	OO	LL	OF	BB	TR
XX	SS	UN	UU	DD	KS	LL

Why can't two elephants go swimming at the same time?

BECAUSE THEY ONLY HAVE ONE PAIR OF TRUNKS!

WHAT IF MY BUTT WERE A CAR BUMPER?

Oh, no! It's the first day of school and my bumper butt is too heavy to walk with. I have to use a forklift. Can you help me get to school on time?

START

FINISH

DAD JOKE

Why did I take my dad to school with me today? Crack the code to find out! Put the 13 words into the grid in alphabetical order. Then write the shaded letters in order from top to bottom in the spaces underneath.

SQUID   CATCH   UNITE
HUMAN   GRAND
ALLOW   ZEBRA   QUIPS
INPUT   TOUGH
OCEAN   BEACH   FRAME

Why did I take my dad to school with me today?

W E   H A D

A   P O P

Q U I Z!

GOT GAS?

My butt is gas-powered! Here's a list of 24 things that can be gas-powered, too. Can you put them all into the grid? They'll fit in only one way. Use the number of letters in each word as a clue to where it might fit. I did one to get you started. When you're done, write the shaded letters, in order from top to bottom, in the spaces to answer my riddle!

3 Letters
SUV
~~VAN~~

4 Letters
LIMO

6 Letters
JET SKI

7 Letters
SCOOTER

8 Letters
CHAIN SAW

9 Letters
BLOWTORCH
GENERATOR
HOUSEBOAT
LAWN MOWER
MOTOR HOME
RACING CAR
SPEEDBOAT

10 Letters
HELICOPTER
LEAF BLOWER
MOTORCYCLE
SPACECRAFT
WEEDWACKER

11 Letters
PICKUP TRUCK
PONTOON BOAT

12 Letters
HEDGE TRIMMER
STATION WAGON

14 Letters
CONVERTIBLE CAR
PROPELLER PLANE

48

What is a 10-letter word that starts with GAS?

_ _ _ _ _ _ _ _ _ _

49

SPACE OUT!

I'm launching into outer space in search of lunar laughs. You can come, too! Use this secret space code to fill in the letters and find the answers to these far-out jokes.

SPACE CODE

   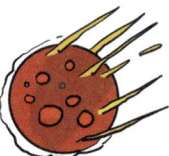

A   B   C   E

   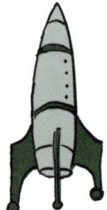

F   G   H   I

K   L   M   N

O   R   S   T

1. How does a space alien count to 25?

___ ___   ___ ___ ___   ___ ___ ___ ___ ___ ___

2. What did the astronaut get when she went mini golfing?

___ ___ ___ ___ ___ ___ ___ - ___ ___ ___ ___

___ ___ ___ ___ ___

3. What do planets like to read?

___ ___ ___ ___   ___ ___ ___ ___ ___ ___

4. How do you say hello to a two-headed space alien?
"___ ___ ___ ___ ___ , ___ ___ ___ ___ ___ !"

BEST OF THE BUNCH

Which of these balloon-butts is the right butt? Find the one picture that matches the real me.

GOTTA RUN!

It's the day of the big race! Will my butt finish first? Follow the paths to see who comes in 1st, 2nd, 3rd, and 4th.

WHAT'S MY BUTT UP TO NEXT?

I'm dreaming about my next big adventure! Draw what you think it is.

ANSWERS

PAGE 3
IT KNOWS HOW TO "CRACK" THE CODE!

PAGE 4

PAGE 5
The match is 3.

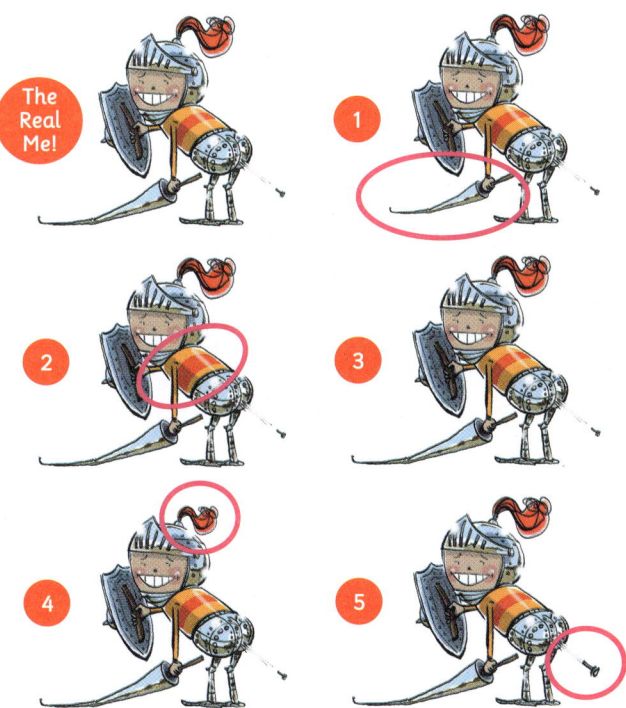

PAGE 7
1. JURASSIC BARK
2. CHASE PARKED CARS
3. PAW-PAW
4. "ROUGH, ROUGH!"

PAGE 9

PAGE 10
1. SUN
2. HEN
3. NUT
4. TUNA
5. AUNT
6. SEAT
7. DUET
8. RAIN
9. STAR
10. UNDER
11. HEART
12. TRAIN
13. TRASH
14. SQUARE
15. THUNDER

PAGE 11

Path 6 is the correct path.

PAGES 12–13

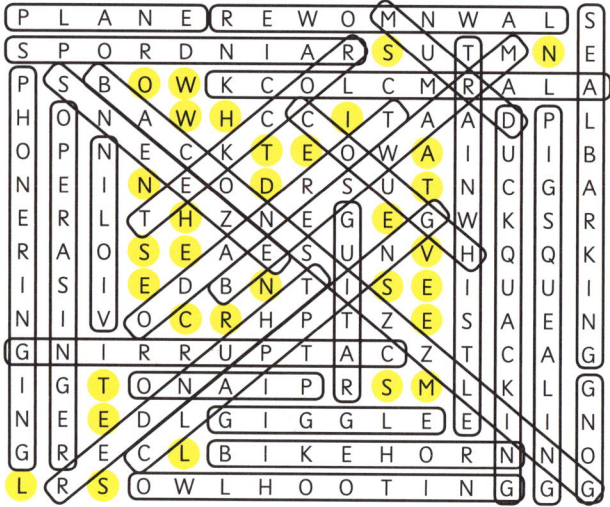

Answer: SNOW WHITE AND THE SEVEN SECRET SMELLS

PAGES 16–17

1. ROUND
5. DOG
7. GRANDMA
13. APRIL
17. LEMON
21. NOSE
24. ELEPHANT
31. TWENTY
36. YEAR
39. RABBIT
44. TOMATO
49. OCEAN
53. NOVEMBER
60. RAISINS
66. SHEEP
70. PARIS
74. SATURDAY
81. YESTERDAY
89. YAWN
92. NEPTUNE
98. EGG

PAGE 18

PAGE 19

PAGE 20

ROCKY ROAD

PAGE 21

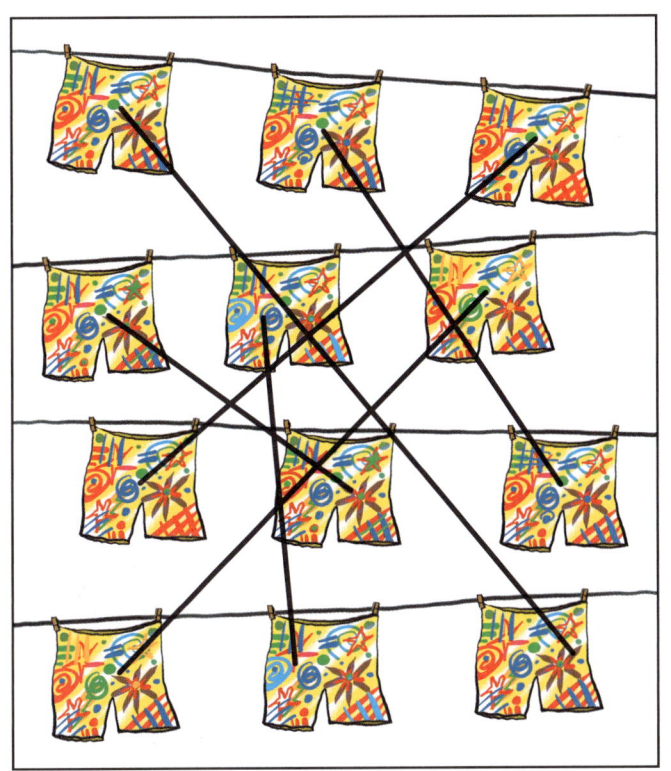

PAGE 22

1. ATTIC
2. LITTLE
3. BETTER
4. KITTEN
5. BUTTER
6. LITTER
7. CATTLE
8. COTTON
9. KETTLE
10. LETTERS
11. MITTENS
12. BUTTONS

PAGE 23

A. 3
B. 5
C. 1
D. 8
E. 2
F. 7
G. 6
H. 4

PAGES 24–25

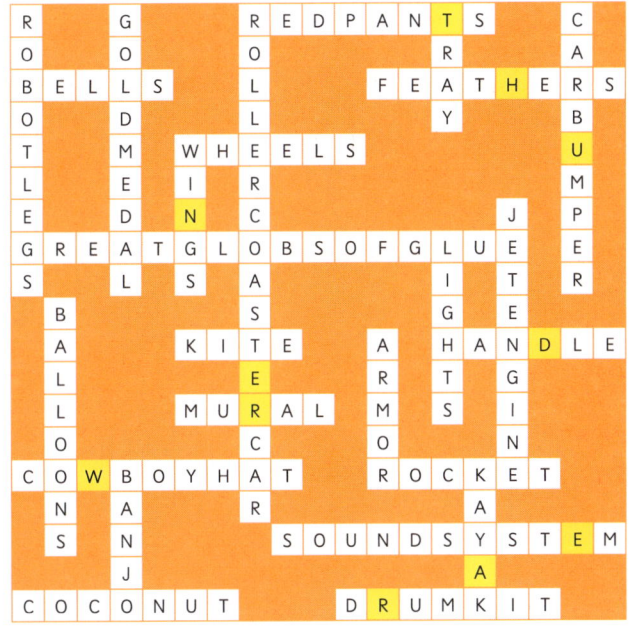

Answer: THUNDER-WEAR!

PAGES 26–27

PAGES 30–31

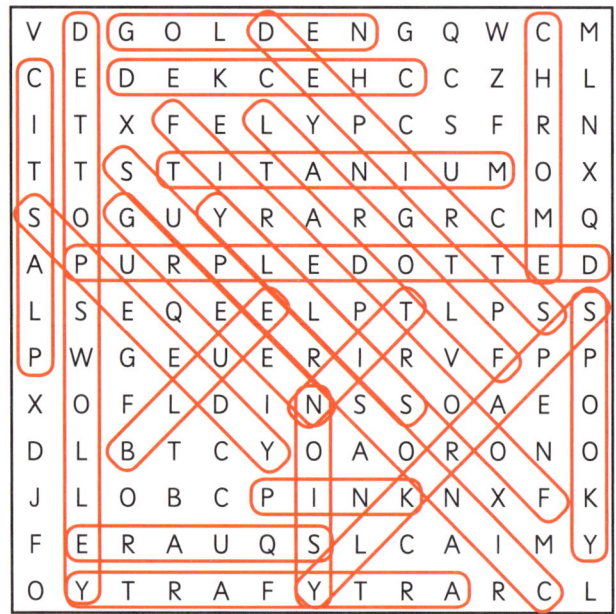

PAGE 32
WHAT DO YOU CALL A DUCK THAT SMELLS BAD?
A FOUL FOWL!

PAGE 33

PAGE 34
Path 5 is the correct path.

PAGE 35
1st Tom, chicken noodle soup
2nd Alexander, tuna surprise
3rd Cam, ham
4th Ben, stew

PAGES 36–37

Bonus activity answer:

PAGE 38
1. PIE
2. TOP
3. TOES
4. ROSE
5. POOR
6. STEP
7. POST
8. TRIO
9. TIRE
10. TROOP
11. SPORT
12. STORE
13. POSTER
14. STRIPE
15. ROOSTER

PAGE 39

A. 6   E. 2
B. 3   F. 4
C. 1   G. 5
D. 8   H. 7

PAGE 40

Dog is knitting the teddy bear.

PAGES 41–42

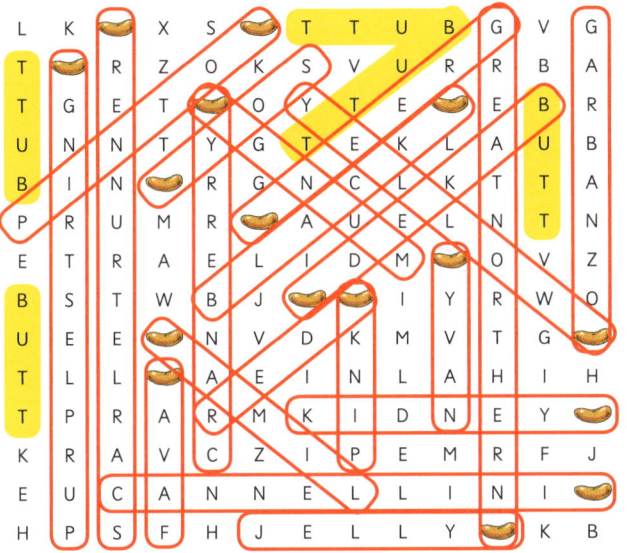

PAGE 43

BUTTOCKS	BUTTOCKS	BUTTOCKS	BUTTOCKS
BUTTOCKS	BUTTOCKS	BUTTOCKS	BUTTOCKS
BUTTOCKS	BUTTOCKS	BUTTOCKS	BUTTOCKS
BUTTOCKS	BUTTOCKS	BUTTOCKS	BUTTOCKS
BUTTOCKS	BUTTOCKS	BUTTOCKS	**BOTTOCKS**
BUTTOCKS	BUTTOCKS	BUTTOCKS	BUTTOCKS
BUTTOCKS	BUTTOCKS	BUTTOCKS	BUTTOCKS
BUTTOCKS	BUTTOCKS	BUTTOCKS	BUTTOCKS
BUTTOCKS	BUTTOCKS	BUTTOCKS	BUTTOCKS
BUTTOCKS	BUTTOCKS	BUTTOCKS	BUTTOCKS
BUTTOCKS	BUTTOCKS	BUTTOCKS	BUTTOCKS
BUTTOCKS	BUTTOCKS	BUTTOCKS	BUTTOCKS
BUTTOCKS	BUTTOCKS	**BUTTCCKS**	BUTTOCKS
BUTTOCKS	BUTTOCKS	BUTTOCKS	BUTTOCKS
BUTTOCKS	BUTTOCKS	BUTTOCKS	BUTTOCKS
BUTTOCKS	BUTTOCKS	BUTTOCKS	BUTTOCKS
BUTTOCKS	BUTTOCKS	BUTTOCKS	BUTTOCKS
BUTTOCKS	BUTTOCKS	BUTTOCKS	BUTTOCKS
BUTTOCHS	BUTTOCKS	BUTTOCKS	BUTTOCKS
BUTTOCKS	BUTTOCKS	BUTTOCKS	BUTTOCKS

PAGE 44

A SCREENSAVER!

PAGE 45

BECAUSE THEY ONLY HAVE ONE PAIR OF TRUNKS!

PAGE 46

PAGE 47

A	L	L	O	**W**
B	**E**	A	C	**H**
C	A	T	C	**H**
F	R	A	M	E
G	R	A	N	**D**
H	U	M	**A**	N
I	N	**P**	U	T
O	C	E	A	N
Q	U	I	**P**	S
S	**Q**	U	I	D
T	O	U	G	H
U	N	I	**T**	E
Z	E	B	R	A

Answer: WE HAD A POP QUIZ!

PAGE 48

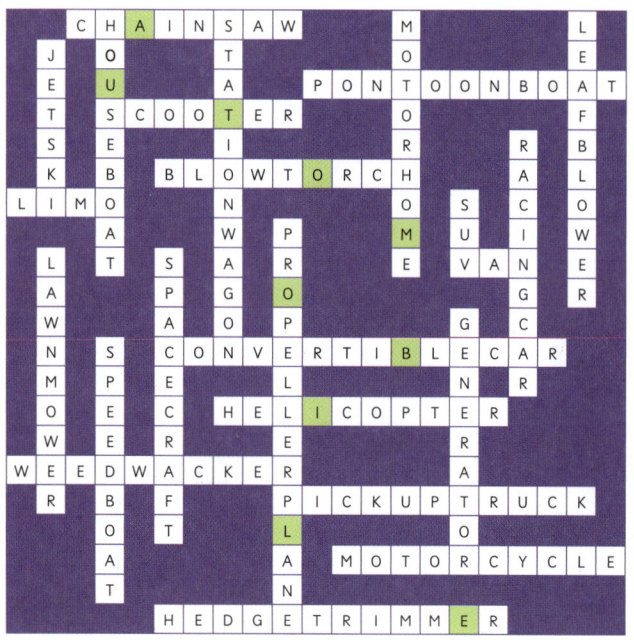

Answer: AUTOMOBILE

PAGES 50–51

1. ON ITS FINGERS
2. A BLACK-HOLE IN ONE
3. COMET BOOKS
4. "HELLO, HELLO!"

PAGE 52

The match is 4.

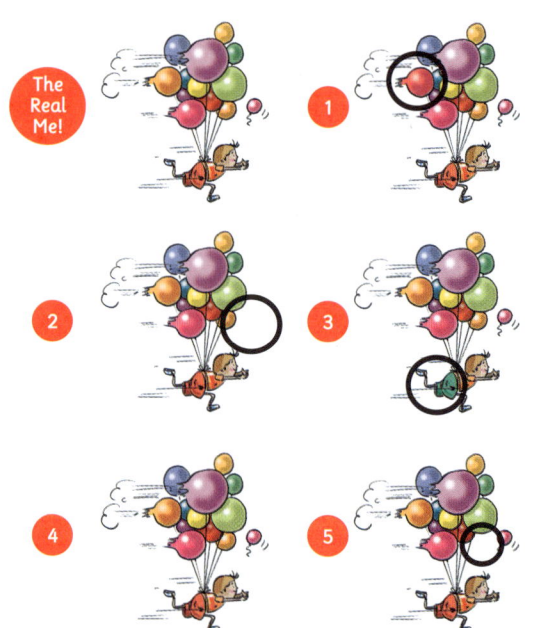

PAGE 53

Dog is 1st
Red pants boy is 2nd
Blue pants boy is 3rd
Pink pants girl is 4th

MAKE A DOOR HANGER!

1. Cut out each door hanger shape on this page and the next one.
2. Trace one onto a piece of cardboard and cut that out.
3. Glue each image onto one side of the cardboard cutout.
4. *Voilà!* You have a door hanger.

MY BUTT IS SO NOISY!

KNOCK LOUDLY!